For Tom and Moppet   J.T.

For Emily Marshall and Trixie   R.C.

Text © 1987 Judy Taylor
Illustrations © 1987 Reg Cartwright

Aladdin Books
Macmillan Publishing Company
866 Third Avenue, New York, NY 10022
First published 1987 in Great Britain by Walker Books Ltd., London
First American edition 1988
First Aladdin Books edition 1989

Printed in Hong Kong by Sheck Wah Tong Printing Press Ltd.

A hardcover edition of *My Cat* is available from Macmillan Publishing Company.

10 9 8 7 6 5 4 3 2 1

Library of Congress Cataloging-in-Publication Data

Taylor, Judy, date.
My cat.
Summary: A little boy describes the activities of his cat from the time
she is a kitten until she has kittens of her own.
[1. Cats—Fiction] I. Cartwright, Reg, ill. II. Title.
PZ7.T21476My 1989   [E]   88–22137
ISBN 0–689–71209–X (pbk.)

My Cat

Written by
Judy Taylor

Illustrated by
Reg Cartwright

Aladdin Books

MACMILLAN PUBLISHING COMPANY

NEW YORK

My cat came as a kitten...

and she was beautiful.

My cat soon got to know me…

and I played with her.

My cat lapped up her milk...

and grew stronger.

My cat was chased
up a tree...

and got stuck there.

My cat scratched our best chair...

and was scolded.

My cat caught a mouse...

and then lost it.

My cat slept all day...

and then went prowling.

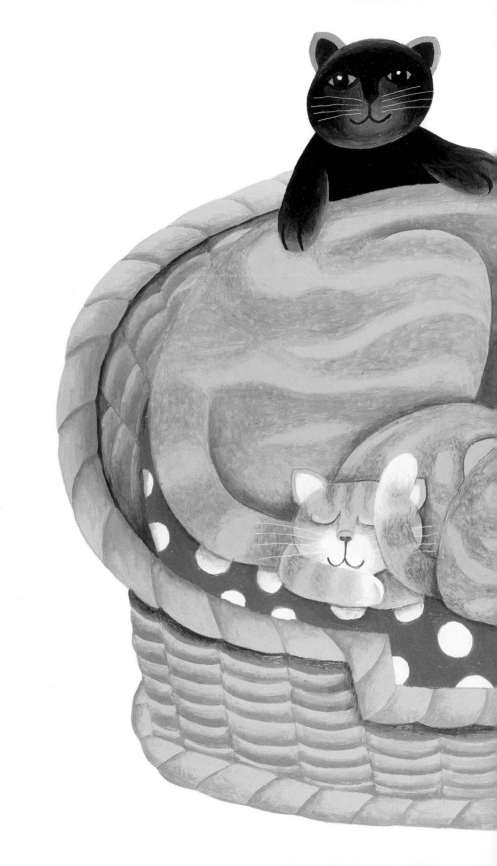

My cat had four tiny kittens...
and she loved them.